DATE DUE

NOV 26			
MAY 18			
JAN 28 '74	Rebecca Cox		16
FEB 11 '74	William Lange		22
	Jenny		5
			31
	Sheila Steward		23
	Diane Smith		27

Fic
W

Williams, Jay
Philbert the Fearful

"The doctor orders Sir Philbert, an appealing but reluctant knight, to rescue the emperor's daughter. When three brave knights fail, Philbert fearfully manages to outwit a giant, a fierce cockatrice and an evil enchanter, and wins the hand of the princess."
— Library Journal

B 14-798

PHILBERT THE FEARFUL

Jay Williams

Philbert the Fearful

ILLUSTRATIONS BY IB OHLSSON

W · W · NORTON & COMPANY INC · NEW YORK

This book
is for my friend
India Tresselt
with love

SIR PHILBERT FITZHUGH was not very brave. This wouldn't have mattered if he had been a mailman or a mason or a mouse-catcher, but he was a knight. Other knights went riding out to slay dragons or rescue princesses, but Sir Philbert stayed comfortably at home taking care of his health. In the summer he looked after his fields and saw to the haying or went for rides on his horse, Roland. In the winter, while other knights wandered through snowstorms or slept in their armor in the cold mud, Philbert curled up by the fire with a good book and an apple.

"After all," he said, "I am the only one of me I have, and I have to take care of myself."

Everyone said, "Knights ought to be brave as lions."

"Maybe so," replied Sir Philbert. "But *I* think it's more important to keep your health." And he went back to his reading and his fire and his apple. "An apple a day," he added, "keeps the doctor away."

Nevertheless, the doctor came.

He came one day and had dinner, and he poked Sir Philbert in the chest and looked at his tongue and felt his pulse. Then he shook his head.

"You're getting flabby," he said. "You ought to get more exercise."

Sir Philbert said, "But I ride for an hour a day."

"Not enough," the doctor said sternly. "Look at yourself! You're pale. You've got the beginnings of a pot-belly. I recommend a good, long trip, plenty of fresh air, activity, a change of scene."

"But I get so seasick," Sir Philbert protested.

The doctor snorted. "Fiddlesticks! Tomorrow morning," said he, "three bold knights are going to search for the emperor's daughter, who has been kidnapped by the enchanter, Brasilgore. I order you to go with them. The adventure will be the best thing for you."

"I?" Sir Philbert became even paler. "Oh, no. No indeed. I couldn't possibly do that. I have too much to do here. I'll stay home and do bending and stretching exercises. I'll ride for *two* hours a day. But I won't go wandering about looking for the emperor's daughter. Let him look for his own daughter."

The next morning at half-past four, the three bold knights started out on their quest. With them was a fourth knight, not so bold. It was Sir Philbert.

He had plenty of warm blankets rolled up behind his saddle. He had plenty of food and medicine in his saddlebags. But he was far from happy.

The other three knights, however, were perfectly happy. They were named Sir Hugo of Brandish, Sir

Armet of Anguish, and Sir Brian of Thump. Their armor was rusty and dented from many adventures. In their saddlebags they carried nothing but bread and hard cheese. Their moustaches were as fierce as their talk.

"We'll slay Brasilgore the enchanter, and find the emperor's daughter, or die in the attempt!" roared Sir Brian.

"Then I certainly hope we find her," mumbled Sir Philbert.

Away they rode, followed by the cheers of several people who had nothing else to do. The doctor, who had come to see Sir Philbert off, waved to them and stumped back to bed.

11

They traveled for many days until they came to a wide, sad plain. Nothing grew there but twisted thorn bushes and purple heather. A wind from the north blew steadily over it. They rode and rode through the heather and into the wind, and at noon they came to a tower. It was high and black. It had one window at the top and a door in front which was a good deal higher than a house.

As they gazed up at it, wondering what it was, a maiden put her head out of the window.

"Help, help!" she cried.

Sir Brian shaded his eyes. "Are you a prisoner?" he called.

"Yes, I am. Please go away," said the maiden.

"Eh?" Sir Brian looked puzzled. "But you just said, help, help."

"Oh, dear, I know I did. I'm sorry. I said help, help, but I meant, go away."

"But why?" asked Sir Hugo of Brandish.

Just then the enormous door opened. "That's why," said the maiden. "Alas, alas, this is the end of you. Goodbye."

Out stepped a giant a good deal higher than a house. He drew a deep breath, stretched, and yawned. It sounded like a thunderstorm overhead.

Sir Hugo lowered his lance. "Stand back, all of you," he shouted. "This giant is mine!"

He rode straight at the giant's ankle. He thrust his lance into the ankle.

"Oh, well done," said Sir Brian.

The giant uttered a yell, "Hornets!" He stamped his foot angrily. Sir Hugo disappeared.

"Adventures!" groaned Sir Philbert. "I just wish that rotten doctor were here."

The other two knights stared uneasily at each other and then at the giant who was leaning against his house and rubbing his ankle, grumbling like an earthquake.

Sir Philbert quickly unfastened his big roll of blankets. He shook them out. He turned his horse and began to gallop away, letting the blankets stream behind him like banners.

The giant saw Sir Philbert and made a giant stride to mash him. Sir Philbert let go of the blankets. They blew away in the endless wind. They flew up and plastered themselves over the giant's eyes. He missed his footing, stumbled on a rock, and fell on his head with a crash. Since he was so much bigger and heavier than an ordinary person, he fell with a far bigger and heavier crash. It was the end of him.

Sir Armet and Sir Brian trotted over and stared at the giant's body. They shook their heads.

"Listen," said Sir Armet, "I don't think that was very sporting."

Palmdale School Library
Phoenix, Arizona 85040

"It was nothing but an accident," Sir Brian agreed. "Philbert didn't kill the giant. He killed himself."

"Yes, I suppose he did," said Sir Philbert. He opened his helmet and mopped his forehead. "But I came on this quest for my health, you know. It wouldn't have been very healthy to go the way poor Hugo went, now would it?"

The maiden came running out of the tower. Sir Philbert took off his helmet, for he was always very polite.

"I'm glad to say you are no longer a prisoner, Miss," he said.

"Oh, thank you," smiled the maiden, who had large, merry brown eyes and long brown hair in two braids down her back. "I'll just get my things, if you'll wait a minute."

"What?" huffed Sir Brian. "Get your things?"

"Of course. I'm coming with you. You rescued me, didn't you?"

"You can't come with us," said Sir Armet. "It's much too dangerous."

"Besides, we haven't an extra horse," said Sir Brian.

"She can ride with me," Sir Philbert said. "We can't leave her here alone, can we?"

The maiden smiled at him. She ran into the tower
and soon returned with four large bundles. They hung
the bundles on Sir Philbert's horse, and Sir Philbert
said it was just as well his blankets had all blown away.
Then the maiden — whose name was Victoria — got up
behind, and away they rode once more, Sir Brian in the
lead, Sir Armet next, and Sir Philbert and Victoria in
the rear.

Victoria said, "I was watching from the window.
Did you really expect those blankets to fly up over the
giant's face?"

Sir Philbert sighed. "I hoped so," he said.

"If they hadn't, what would you have done?"

"I would have kept on riding as fast as I could. I didn't see how else I could beat a giant that tall."

"But shouldn't a knight be brave?"

"Oh, yes," said Sir Philbert. "But on the other hand, I'm the only one of me I have, and I have to take care of myself."

Victoria nodded. "That's reasonable," she said. "But what about me?"

"I'll have to take care of you too, I guess," said Sir Philbert. And he sighed again.

They rode on and on, and after a time the ground became steeper. The plain rose before them in low, stony hills. Then great ragged rocks appeared, and the air became colder. The heather and thorn bushes were gone. There was nothing but stone, black and hard, that rang with frost under the horses' iron shoes.

At last they came to the highest place of all. The road ran over a peak that sparkled with glassy ice. On each side, the rock fell away in steep cliffs, down, down,

to glittering rock below. Sir Brian's horse suddenly reared and skittered round. Sir Armet joined him and his horse reared too. After a bit Sir Philbert and Victoria caught up with them and saw what they saw. Their horse couldn't rear because it was too heavily loaded, but it planted its legs hard and began to shiver.

There was a cockatrice in the way. It had the body of a serpent and the head and legs of a rooster. Its scales were green and shiny in the icy light. Its long serpent tongue flicked in and out of its cock's beak, and its round, evil eyes rolled forward to look at them. It strutted as tall as a man on its scaly legs.

"Hmm," said Sir Philbert. "Do we have to go this way?"

Sir Brian snapped, "Yes, we do. Would you like the honor of attacking the beast?"

"It might be better to go back and find another way," Sir Philbert murmured. "After all, we have a lady with us."

"Pah! You are a coward, sir," said Sir Armet. "Stand back, all of you."

He lowered his lance and galloped forward.

"Oh, dear," Sir Philbert whispered to Victoria. "I really don't think he has a chance."

Sir Armet's lance shattered on the green scales. The cockatrice hissed. It darted its rooster's beak forward on its snaky neck. Sir Armet's horse gave a scream and leaped aside. It plunged over the edge of the cliff with Sir Armet and a few pebbles.

"Stand back, all of you," said Sir Brian slowly and rather nervously. He began to lower his lance. But Sir Philbert caught hold of his elbow.

"Wait a minute," said Sir Philbert. "I just thought of something I'd like to try."

He got off his horse. "Victoria, my dear," he said, "have you a mirror?"

"Oh, yes," she answered. She opened one of her bundles and took out a large, golden looking glass with her initial "V" in emeralds on the back. "Please be careful with it," she said. "I got it for my birthday."

Sir Philbert took it and walked forward, his armor squeaking and clinking in the still, cold air. The cockatrice shot out its fearsome head once again. Sir Philbert held out the mirror.

The cockatrice stared into it. Then it gave a dithering hiss of horror, spread its wings, and flew away over the peaks, a green blot that quickly vanished into the pale sky.

Sir Philbert returned the looking glass to Victoria. He was shaking like a leaf.

"Why, how brave of you!" cried Victoria, giving him a hug.

"No, not very brave," said Sir Philbert. "The only thing a cockatrice is afraid of is another cockatrice. I was pretty sure it would fly off when it saw its face in the mirror. I read that in a book," he added humbly.

"Then it was very clever of you," Victoria said firmly, giving him another hug.

"Hmph!" grunted Sir Brian. "Clever? I'm not so sure a knight *ought* to be clever."

Sir Philbert hung his head. "I know. But you see, I'm the only one of me I have . . . ."

"Suppose we have a bite of lunch and then push on," Sir Brian said briskly.

When they had finished eating, they followed the road over the top of the mountain and down the other side. That night they rested beside a warm, tinkling stream in a green and pleasant valley. Next morning, they set out riding through the woods. After a time, Sir Philbert remarked, "These trees are growing in rows, almost like a park."

"Rubbish!" said Sir Brian. "It's a wild wood."

"There's no underbrush either," Sir Philbert continued. "Just smooth grass between the tree trunks. It really is like a park."

"Ridiculous!" said Sir Brian. "Next you'll be telling me you see a castle."

"I see a castle," Sir Philbert said.

Sure enough, the trees ended at a bridge, and on the other side of it there was a gloomy castle with many turrets and spires.

"Ha!" Sir Brian exclaimed. "The castle of the enchanter!"

"Are you sure?" asked Sir Philbert.

"Of course I'm sure. Don't you think I know what an enchanter's castle looks like?" Sir Brian retorted.

They rode across the bridge and under a gateway like a giant's yawn, into a paved courtyard. Nobody came. All was silent.

Sir Brian rubbed his hands together. "Now then," he said, "the enchanter is probably upstairs in his den. I'll go after him. If anything happens to me — which isn't very likely because I know how to handle these fellows — just remember one rule. You must hold on to the enchanter until he surrenders. He will turn himself into all sorts of beasts: a lion, a wolf, a dragon, anything. As long as you hold him you're safe. If you let go of him, he'll magic you, and — *poof!*"

Sir Philbert nodded. "I've read all about that in . . ." he began, but Sir Brian was gone. He had gone with a firm stride, sword in hand, into the castle.

Sir Philbert rubbed his chin. "You know," he said to Victoria, "I'm not at all sure this is the right castle. I'm not even sure it's an enchanter's castle."

"Never mind," said Victoria.

"But I *do* mind. I think I'd better follow Brian. Suppose something happens to him?"

"Suppose something happens to you?" said Victoria.

"Don't let's talk about it," Sir Philbert gulped.

He walked into the castle. There was a large cobwebby hall with a winding, dusty stair at one end of it. He could see Sir Brian's footprints in the dust. He began to follow them.

Now Sir Brian had climbed the stairs, and he had
found, at the top, a heavy door opening into a tower
room. Inside, there was a little old man with a bristle of
untidy hair like a used broom full of dust or a dried
chrysanthemum. Sir Brian sprang in and seized him
by the neck.

"Ha, foul wizard," shouted Sir Brian, "I have thee!"

The old man at once turned into a lion. Sir Brian held fast. The lion became a fanged wolf. Sir Brian with a laugh still held him. The wolf became a dragon. Sir Brian held on. The dragon, in the blink of an eye, turned into a lady.

"Oh, you're hurting me," said the lady. "Not very knightly of you."

"I beg your pardon," said Sir Brian. He let go at once. The enchanter promptly waved his hand and turned Sir Brian into a pelican, which gave a dismal squawk and flew out the window.

The enchanter changed back into himself and began to dust off his cloak. At that instant, Sir Philbert, who

had seen the whole thing from the doorway, rushed in and grabbed the enchanter by the neck.

"What? Another one?" shrieked the enchanter in annoyance.

He was so confused that he turned himself into a dreadful combination of lion, wolf, dragon, and woman all at once. Sir Philbert gritted his teeth and hung on.

The enchanter then turned into a unicorn, a falcon, a salmon, a chest of drawers, a saber-toothed tiger, and a burning wastepaper basket. Sir Philbert held on for dear life. At last, the enchanter turned into a wasp. This time, Sir Philbert almost did let go. But he thought of his health and of Victoria and of poor blus-

tering Sir Brian, who was now a pelican, and he
gripped the wasp tightly. It didn't sting him after all.
Instead, it turned back into the enchanter, looking
more untidy than ever and extremely sulky.

"Very well," he panted. "You've won. What is your
wish?"

"I want you to take the spell off Sir Brian," said Sir Philbert.

"What, right now?"

"At once."

The enchanter chuckled disagreeably. "Very well," he said. He waved his hand. Sir Brian, who was at that moment flying low over a swamp, changed back into himself and fell plop! into the mud.

"Your friend is himself again," said the enchanter.
"Anything else?"

"Yes," said Sir Philbert, remembering the reason for
the quest. "I want you to let the emperor's daughter
go."

"Let her go? How can I let her go when I haven't got
her?"

"Oh, my," groaned Sir Philbert. "I knew it was the
wrong castle. Well, who did kidnap her?"

"She was kidnapped by Brasilgore," said the enchanter. "And she has already been rescued."

"She has? Where is she?"

"Downstairs in my courtyard," snarled the enchanter. "Now, if there's nothing else I can do for you, will you please go away?"

But Sir Philbert had already gone, down the stairs two at a time.

"And so Brasilgore the enchanter was a giant," he said as he and Victoria went trotting off together, she riding more comfortably on Sir Brian's horse. "But why didn't you tell us?"

"You never asked me," Victoria replied.

"That's true. Well, I suppose I'd better take you home to your father as quickly as possible."

They traveled until they came to the emperor's empire. They entered the great city, and all the people ran out to cheer and stare and point. They came to the castle, and there was the emperor on a throne of ivory and emeralds. There also was Sir Brian, looking very muddy and rusty and bothered.

"Victoria, my darling, I'm so glad to see you again," said the emperor, embracing her. "Sir Brian was telling me how he had failed to find you."

Victoria hugged her father. "I must just tell you everything that has happened," she cried. And so she did.

When she was finished, the emperor said, "I have sworn to give half my kingdom and my daughter's hand to the man brave enough to rescue her."

Sir Philbert blushed. "My lord," he said, "I really don't want half your kingdom. I have a nice little castle of my own, and it's all I can do to manage it."

"Oho. Is that so?" said the emperor.

"Yes, my lord. But — but I *would* rather like to have Victoria," said Sir Philbert.

Victoria smiled and took his hand.

Then Sir Brian interrupted. "My lord emperor," he

cried, "that man didn't rescue your daughter by bravery.
He killed the giant by accident and the cockatrice by a
trick."

"Dear me," said the emperor.He stroked his beard
thoughtfully. "Now let me get this straight. Where is
Sir Hugo of Brandish?"

"He died a hero's death, sire," said Sir Brian.

"I see. And Sir Armet of Anguish?"

"Perished bravely in combat."

"Ah. And as for you, you'd still be a pelican if it
hadn't been for Sir Philbert, eh?"

Sir Brian frowned. "But he is a coward!" he said.

"Ah, yes, there's that." The emperor turned to one of his servants and whispered in his ear. The servant turned pale and ran off. He came back in a few moments with a large box. From the box came a loud and angry humming. The servant had several bumps on his face as well as a woeful look.

"Now, gallant sirs," said the emperor, "here is a box containing a wasps' nest. I'd like one of you to reach

inside and catch a wasp for me and to hold it up in your
fingers. There is no reward. I just happen to want a
wasp."

The knights and barons of the court looked at one
another. They looked at the box and at the unhappy
servant who was holding it. Sir Brian reached out a
hand, listened to the furious humming, winced, and
drew it back. Nobody else moved.

"You see," said the emperor, "when Sir Philbert held on to the enchanter he was being quite as brave as was necessary. Sir Philbert, will you reach in and get me a wasp?"

Sir Philbert swallowed hard. He had had more practice than anyone else, so to speak, but he didn't much want to do it again. Then, suddenly, he had an idea. He grinned. He pulled on one of his iron gloves, reached into the box, and took out a wasp. Of course, it couldn't sting him through the iron.

Victoria laughed. She said to her father, "He's the only one of him there is, and I'm the only one of me there is, and he knows how to take care of both of us."

"Quite right," said the emperor. "I'd much rather have my daughter married to someone with sense enough to stay alive and take care of her than have her married to a pelican."

46

So Philbert and Victoria were married and rode happily home.

"And do you know the second best thing about the whole adventure?" beamed Sir Philbert as they rode into their own courtyard. "I did get some exercise and I did lose some weight."

"And what was the first best thing?" asked Victoria, although she knew.

"You were, my dear," said Sir Philbert fondly. "You were just what the doctor ordered."

THE AUTHOR

Jay Williams is the author of numerous books for children and adults. His books for young readers range from non-fiction (*Augustus Caesar, Knights of the Crusades*) to fiction stories such as *The Stolen Oracle* and *The Sword and the Scythe*. Mr. Williams is also co-author with Raymond Abrashkin of the popular Danny Dunn science-fiction series. His stories, articles and poems have appeared in such diverse publications as *The American Scholar, Esquire, The Saturday Evening Post,* and *Fantasy and Science Fiction.*

A native of Buffalo, New York, Mr. Williams has lived in West Redding, Connecticut, for the past eighteen years, with occasional time off for living abroad, as he did in 1963. During World War II, he served with the 65th infantry and was wounded in Germany. In 1949, Mr. Williams received a Guggenheim Fellowship. Jay Williams is married, and has a son and a daughter.

THE ARTIST

Ib Ohlsson began his art career in Copenhagen, Denmark, where he was born in 1935. He worked for four years as apprentice to a graphic designer there, while at the same time attending classes at the School of Decorative and Applied Arts.

In 1956, after two years service in the Danish Civil Defense, Mr. Ohlsson opened his own studio in Copenhagen. He specialized in graphic arts and advertising design and later began illustrating textbooks as well. During that time he traveled extensively throughout Germany, France, Switzerland, Italy, Spain, and Morocco.

Ib Ohlsson made his first trip to the United States in 1950 on a student grant. He returned here in 1960 and now lives with his wife and small son in Kew Gardens, New York.